DINOSAURS' CHRISTMAS

by Liza Donnelly

SCHOLASTIC INC./New York

For Ella

With special thanks to Dr. Eugene Gaffney, Curator, Department
of Vertebrate Paleontology from the American Museum of
Natural History, for fact-checking the glossary.

A LUCAS • EVANS BOOK

Liza Donnelly uses waterproof black ink and either a rapidiograph or quill pen.
Paints are a concentrated watercolor called dyes.

Copyright © 1991 by Liza Donnelly.
All rights reserved. Published by Scholastic Inc.
SCHOLASTIC HARDCOVER is a registered trademark of Scholastic Inc.

No part of this publication may be reproduced in whole or in
part, or stored in a retrieval system, or transmitted in any
form or by any means, electronic, mechanical, photocopying,
recording, or otherwise, without written permission of the publisher.
For information regarding permission, write to
Scholastic Inc., 730 Broadway, New York, New York 10003.

Library of Congress Cataloging-in-Publication Data
Donnelly, Liza.
Dinosaurs' Christmas / by Liza Donnelly.
p.   cm.
Summary: Rex finds trouble at the North Pole. The elves are making the
dinosaurs all wrong and all the reindeer have the flu. Can Rex save
Christmas?
ISBN 0-590-44797-1
[1. Dinosaurs—Fiction. 2. Christmas—Fiction] I. Title.
PZ7.D7195Dhr 1991 [E]—dc20 90-23090 CIP AC

12 11 10 9 8 7 6 5 4 3 2 1   1 2 3 4 5 6/9
Printed in the U.S.A   36
First Scholastic printing, October 1991

"Bones! Let's go sledding!"

"Did you know that dinosaurs lived before the Ice Ages?"

"The last Ice Age began about one hundred thousand years ago. And the early dinosaurs lived about two hundred million years ago!"

"This is a good hill."

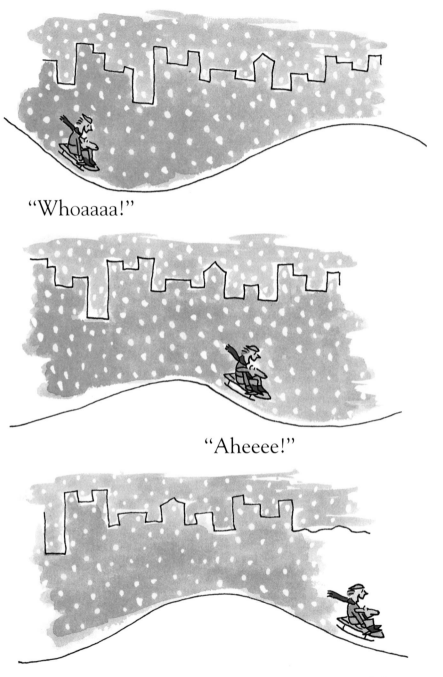

"Whoaaaa!"

"Aheeee!"

"Aaaaahh!"

"Eeeee!"

"Ooooh!"

"Yikes!"

"It's . . .

. . . a Plateosaurus!"

*"Hi!"

"Where are we?"   *"The North Pole."

*"There's trouble in Santa's workshop and they need your help."

*"Santa's helpers are making toy dinosaurs."

"And look, Bones, they're making them all wrong!"

"Wait!"

"Let me help!"

"This Othnielia did not have a beak, but a round nose."

"While the Pteranodon *did* have a large beak!"

"This Nodosaurus didn't have wings."

"Bactrosaurus had only one tail!"

"And the Kentrosaurus had many spikes,
but not on its face."

"It's late — I wonder where Santa is?"

"The reindeer all have the flu!"

"How are we going to get the toys to all the kids?
It's impossible if Santa can't fly!"

"My friend Plateosaurus will help."

"Now Plateosaurus! Now Pteranodon!
Now Nodosaurus! And Pentaceratops!"

"On Bactrosaurus! On Stegoceras!
On Kentrosaurus and Othnielia!"

"Merry Christmas!"

"Wow!"

"This was the best Christmas ever!"

GLOSSARY

BACTROSAURUS (BAK-truh-sawr-us) *Staff lizard.* This plant-eater was one of the earliest known duck-billed dinosaurs. Scientists don't know exactly what its head looked like, but Bactrosaurus did have long hind legs and short forelegs. It was 13 feet long.

KENTROSAURUS (KEN-truh-sawr-us) *Spiked lizard.* Two rows of bony spikes and plates rose along this dinosaurs' back and tail. Kentrosaurus was a plant-eater, and may have used its spiked tail for defense. It was 16 feet long.

NODOSAURUS (no-doe-SAWR-us) *Toothless lizard.* This 18 foot plant-eater had many armored plates on its back. It had a small head but short stout legs. Nodosaurus is one of the earliest known armored dinosaurs.

OTHNIELIA (oth-NEEL-ee-ah) Was named for the scientist who discovered it. A plant-eater, Othnielia was only four feet long and was very light weight. It had long legs, large eyes, and is sometimes called the gazelle of the dinosaur world.

PENTACERATOPS   (PEN-tah-sair-uh-tops) *Five-horned face.*
This dinosaur had five horns; two on its brow, one on its nose,
and one on either cheek. A plant-eater, Pentaceratops's head
was one third the length of its 20-foot body.

PLATEOSAURUS (PLAY-tee-uh-sawr-us) *Flat lizard.*
At 23 feet, this plant-eater usually walked on all fours, but
may have reared on its two hind legs to feed from treetops.
"Flat lizard" refers to Plateosaurus's flat teeth.

PTERANODON (tair-AN-o-don) *Winged and toothless.* One of
the largest Pterosaurs, Pteranodon was probably a glider. The
function of its great crest is unknown. It had no teeth and may
have caught fish by scooping them up like a pelican. It had a
23-foot wing span. It was not a dinosaur.

STEGOCERAS   (steg-OSS-air-us) *Covered horn.* The whole body of this
dinosaur seemed designed to provide the power behind its ramming head.
It was a plant-eater, bipedal, and only six feet long.

ICE AGES   Periods of time in which climates were colder than at present,
and vast areas were covered with snow and glaciers.